Letter to Pluto

To Lucy,
who was the first
to go to Pluto

Letter to Pluto
An original concept by author Lou Treleaven
© Lou Treleaven

Illustrations by Lou Treleaven
Cover illustrations by Katie Abey

MAVERICK ARTS PUBLISHING LTD
Studio 11, City Business Centre, 6 Brighton Road,
Horsham, West Sussex, RH13 5BB
+44 (0) 1403 256941
© Maverick Arts Publishing Limited
First published in the UK in 2016 by MAVERICK ARTS
PUBLISHING LTD

American edition published in 2019 by Maverick Arts
Publishing, distributed in the United States and
Canada by Lerner Publishing Group Inc., 241 First
Avenue North, Minneapolis, MN 55401 USA

ISBN: 978-1-84886-470-2

Distributed by **Lerner.**

Letter to Pluto

By Lou Treleaven

WHY NOT VACATION IN...

THE OUTER SOLAR SYSTEM

URANUS!

NEPTUNE!

and Pluto.

URANUS

It's brrrilliant!

The coldest planet in the solar system, Uranus is perfect for your next vacation.

Wrap up warm and give it a try!

Can you escape the deadly Blarg-ringed flapper?

Find out on Neptune!

Come to Neptune's water parks and try some fun sports while weird creatures lurk beneath the waves!

Pluto

Small, smelly, and far away. DON'T BOTHER.

Class 5H

Northcroft School

Northcroft

Earth

Tuesday, January 10th, 2317

Dear Straxi,

Our teacher Mrs. Hall wants us to

write a letter to someone on another

planet. I've got you. I didn't know

anyone even lived on Pluto.

"What's a letter?" I asked Mrs. Hall.

"You need a pen, paper, and an

envelope," Mrs. Hall said. She is writing

to a principal on Mars about ~~nit~~
knitting patterns. I've got nothing to
say about knitting. So Mrs. Hall said
to tell you about my family. "Who'd
want to know about them?" I said, but
Mrs. Hall said I had to get to work or
stay in during recess, so here goes.

MY FAMILY

My big brother. He looks like
this when he's chasing me.
Scary.

Little sis. Always happy.
About everything. No one
knows why.

 Dad. He fixes computers.
He likes taking things apart
for fun.

Mom. Her name is Dawn.
She has a gardening
~~busn~~ business called
Dawn's Lawns. I asked her yesterday
what she would have done for a job if
she hadn't been called Dawn. She gave
me a funny look.

I'm stopping now because my hand is
aching. Mrs. Hall says we have to
keep writing, it is a dying art.

"Good, let it die," I said, and then she said, "You are staying in during recess Jon Fisher."

Jon

Class 5U

Flumpenslurp Blurble School

Dome 1

Pluto

Fiveday, Gagarin 13th, 2317

Dear Jon,

Thank you for your letter. It was funny. I've never had a letter and didn't know what to expect. It wasn't that! You told me all about your family, so here is mine.

STRAXI'S FAMILY

My grandma. She is the principal at my school.

Imagine living with your principal.
Imagine walking to school with your
principal.

Mom and Dad. They run a café
called Doolyboppers, and we live
above it. My dad is well known
because he has a weird
hairstyle that has never caught
on (yet)! Mom's grandparents were the
first people to move to Pluto from Earth.
Their names are carved onto a stone
spaceship in the town square. Fame!

My twin, Bryd. She's always
around. She's even leaning over me as I

write this letter. GO AWAY BRYD!

These are my pets. I have two pimpams
and a striped zork. Actually, I don't
because we can't have pets living above
the café. So I have imaginary pets
instead. They are very well trained,
apart from the zork, which
keeps sitting on my head.

You forgot to draw a picture of yourself.
If you want to know what I look like, look
at the drawing of Bryd. She's just like
me.

Straxi

13

Class 5H

Northcroft School

Northcroft

Earth

Tuesday, January 17th, 2317

Dear Straxi,

Mrs. Hall graded our letters out of
ten for neatness. She gave mine a
four. I thought she'd be pleased to
read all that stuff about herself, but
no. She gave yours a nine.

My grandma would make a very bad
principal. She went planet-hopping
when Grandpa died and enjoys it so

much she hasn't come home yet.

Grandma likes writing by hand just as much as Mrs. Hall and is always sending us postcards that take weeks to get here. The last one was a postcard of a giant snail on Jupiter. By the time we got it, she'd left and gone to Neptune. Dad said the snail could have gotten to us faster than that postcard.

← slime

I don't know how people ever wrote letters like these all the time. My hand is going to fall off, and then Mrs. Hall will be sorry. Mrs. Hall said

that in the old days, they used to
write with quills dipped in ink. The
quills were made out of feathers
sharpened at the end. "Why weren't
the birds all bald, then?" I asked, and
Mrs. Hall told me to stop being so silly
and did I want to miss recess again.

Jon

P.S. Why did you say you looked just
like your twin—she is a girl!

Class 5U

Flumpenslurp Blurble School

Dome 1

Pluto

Fiveday, Gagarin 20th, 2317

Dear Jon,

Of course I am a girl! What did you think I was, a blue-headed skwitch? Do you have them on Earth? We have tons on Pluto. They are giant birds with six foot long feathers—that's one whole dad. I asked my dad to build a birdhouse in the backyard for

one dad

one feather

them, but they squashed
it flat. And him, because
he was underneath it
putting the last nail in.
But he is okay now.

Your grandma sounds great. I'd love to
planet hop. I've never even left Pluto.

I like the idea of writing with a feather.
Did people really do that? And did the
birds go bald in the end? I would have
knitted them sweaters in return. It's
only fair.

Straxi

Class 5H

Northcroft School

Northcroft

Earth

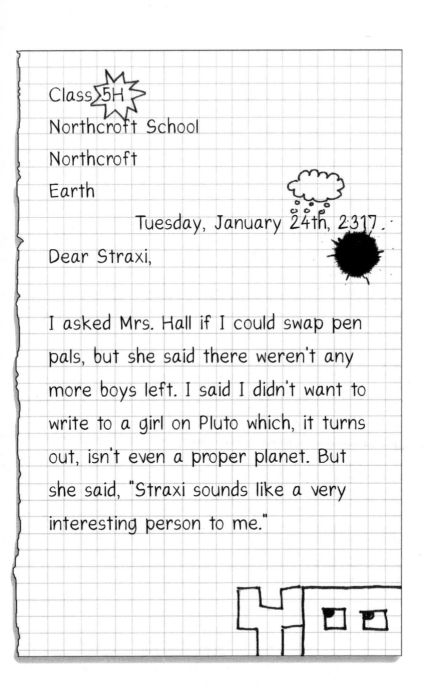

Tuesday, January 24th, 2317.

Dear Straxi,

I asked Mrs. Hall if I could swap pen
pals, but she said there weren't any
more boys left. I said I didn't want to
write to a girl on Pluto which, it turns
out, isn't even a proper planet. But
she said, "Straxi sounds like a very
interesting person to me."

Rex Smith's pen pal collects old
toothbrushes, so perhaps she's right.

Then Mrs. Hall said, "Why don't you
find out a bit more about quills?" so I
did. Then she said, "How interesting,
Jon, why don't you write a report
about it?" and I cursed deep inside
my head where she couldn't hear and
said, "Yeah okay, why not."

So there is a copy of it in the
envelope, and you can read it and
make it into a paper airplane if you
want.

And then Mrs. Hall did a surprising thing—she came up to me with a present. It is a pen that looks like a quill, but it's really a ballpoint pen, and I'm writing with it now!

I'm keeping the quill at school in my desk. If my big brother knew I was writing to a girl on Pluto with a quill, he'd die laughing.

Jon

ha ha ha

A HISTORY OF QUILLS by Jon Fisher

A quill is a pen made out of a feather, which seems a bit random. I mean, why a feather, why not a stick? ✓

Interesting start Jon.

Anyway, turns out there is a reason besides just the nice fluffy parts at the end that flap about making you look like Shakespeare, but also the inside is hollow and filled with ink. ✓ Not while it's on the bird, though, or it wouldn't be able to take off. Also, it could write its name in the sky if it did manage to take off.

What's the difference between a quill and my brother? One is full of ink, and the other (guess which) is full of stink.

Not appropriate Jon.

Quills were really popular in the Middle Ages, ✓ and tons of people had them, especially monks who liked to draw in the margins of their books. That isn't allowed today—rough luck.

Then metal pens were invented and everyone decided they would pay for them and not pick them up for free off the ground, which is weird. Oh, except for some artists who still like writing in old styles for fun.

Remember to keep on the subject!

Quills have levels like baseball teams do, where swan is the top, followed by goose, and right down the list is turkey. ✔ I would like to try writing with a peacock feather—it would be huge and good for big things like billboard signs. *Better...*

If you are right-handed, you should use a feather from a bird's left wing, and if you are left-handed, you should use one from their right wing. ✔ A good way to remember this is to imagine you are shaking hands with a bird.

Lovely picture.

An interesting, if rather short, history of quills.

Try to report the facts rather than your own train of thought. Mrs. Hall.

Class 5U

Flumpenslurp Blurble School

Dome 1

Pluto

Fiveday, Gagarin 27th, 2317

Dear Jon,

I don't know about Earth, but here on
Pluto, you can be friends with anyone.
One of mine and Bryd's best friends is a
boy and he's bright blue. But I guess it's
different on Earth.

I asked Miss Urdlepun—that's my
teacher—if I could swap pen pals too,
but she said there must be something

we have in common, even if we are from different planets.

So I thought hard, and here's a list of things we have in common.

1. We both have pen pals! Okay, that's a bit silly.

2. We both have crazy grandmas. Not everyone does, believe it or not.

3. We both hate vomblefruit. (That's just a guess. But everyone hates vomblefruit, right?)

Pew!

4. We both like quills. Yours sounds cool.
I wish I had one.

Straxi

P.S. I also have an imaginary zork on
my head, but Bryd says that's not
normal.

Class 5H

Northcroft School

Northcroft

Earth

Tuesday, January 31st, 2317

Dear Straxi,

Mrs. Hall liked your list. She said, "Why

don't you write back about that, Jon,

instead of staring into space?" so here

goes.

1. We both have pen pals! So does

everyone in my class. Well, nearly

everyone. Rex Smith got banned. I don't

know what he wrote, but Mrs. Hall tore up

his letter and put in the trash.

2. We both have crazy grandmas. Grandma sent me a photo of her surfing on Neptune wearing a "Hello Earth" T-shirt.

3. We both hate vomblefruit. What is vomblefruit? If everyone hates them then, they sound a bit like brussel evil sprout sprouts, which are the color of puke and evil.

4. We both like quills. If you like quills you will like this because guess what? I am sending you the quill in case my brother

28

finds out about it. Actually, you've probably already seen it in the envelope. So this is the last sentence I will ever write with a quill.

Apart from this one, goodbye.

Jon

(And that one.)

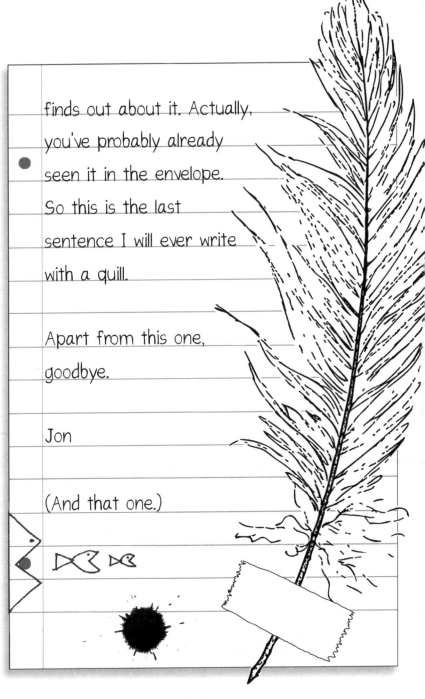

Class 5U

Flumpenslurp Blurble School

Dome 1

Pluto

Fiveday, Fiennes 3rd, 2317

Dear Jon,

Thank you for the quill that I am
writing with right now.

It makes me think I'm in the olden days
on Earth when people lived in castles
and shot arrows at each other (twang!)
and didn't even know Pluto was here.
I would send you a blue-headed skwitch
feather, but they are six feet long (or

about one dad) and hard to fit in an envelope.

So instead, I am sending you a vomblefruit so you can see for yourself how horrible they are.

Make sure you peel it outside so you don't stink everybody out. Then take a bite. A big one!

Straxi

THE VOMBLEFRUIT COOKBOOK

By Ursula Copperbottom

Take the 'vom' out of vomblefruit with these mouth-watering recipes!

Includes:

Vomblefruit pie
Vomblefruit smoothie
Vomblefruit tart with vomblefruit cream
Roast vomblefruit on a bed of vomblefruit
with vomblefruit sauce

You won't believe it's got vomblefruit in it!
(unless you taste it)

The Vomblefruit Cookbook © Ursula Copperbottom
Published by PLUTO PRESS LTD
52, Main Street, Dome 1, Pluto, Outer Solar System
© Pluto Press Ltd. 28th Grylls 2305
ISBN: 978-1-53842-189-2

Class 5H

Northcroft School

Northcroft

Earth

Tuesday, February 7th, 2317

Dear Straxi,

YEEEUUUCHHH! You're right. I hate vomblefruit. I tricked big bro into trying some, to get him back for all the times he chases me around the house pretending to be a monster (he doesn't have to pretend much). He grabbed it right out of my hand and took a huge bite. He now looks like this:

My little sis didn't try the vomblefruit. She still looks like this:

Dad said to bury it, but Mom was worried it would grow into a vomblefruit tree and all our neighbours would collapse from the smell.

So she put it in her greenhouse instead, and now she goes and admires it every day. I suppose it's not bad to look at now that it's too far away to make me barf.

ewl Jon

Class 5U

Flumpenslurp Blurble School

Dome 1

Pluto

Happyday, Fiennes 11th, 2317

Dear Jon,

I'm glad your mom kept the vomblefruit.
Tell her to hold it up in the sunlight to
see the colors at their best. Too bad it
tastes like a snargler's toothbrush.

A snargler is a blind, double-ended slug
thing that lives in swamps. In case you
don't have them on Earth.

I asked Dad why vomblefruit trees don't grow all over Earth, too, and he said Earth is four and a half light hours away and has a completely different eco-system, which means plants and stuff.

But guess what? The President of Pluto is trying to get rid of all the smelly vomblefruit trees so more tourists will come. Then maybe you could visit one day and see blue-headed skwitches and snarglers for yourself!

Here's a leaflet about snarglers for you to read. It was put through the door of the café by someone in a parka.

It's the weekend, so I'm helping out at
Doolyboppers today. Got to go!

Straxi

President of Pluto

Nature walk
and Snargler Count

The society's nature walk will take place next Funday in the Pulsating Swamp. Members will be asked to count how many snarglers they see and record them in their snargler spotters' notebooks. Please bring a parka and a flask of plubberslurp as we will be pausing mid-swamp for a break.

Know your snarglers!

Tick off the ones you've seen!

Common snargler

☐

Southern swamp snargler

☐

Northern swamp snargler

☐

The rare middle swamp snargler

☐

This is not a snargler, this is a link

Class 5H

Northcroft School

Northcroft

Earth

Tuesday, February 21st, 2317

Dear Straxi,

Everyone has gone handwriting crazy
because guess what? WiseUp TV are
coming to school to make a program
about us! They heard about Mrs. Hall and
her mission, and they want to film us all
writing to our pen pals on other planets.

Mrs. Hall went into a real panic, especially
when she thought I'd lost the quill that

panic!

she hoped would look good on TV. When I told her I'd sent it to you, she changed her tune and said, "Jon, you are a surprising boy sometimes," to which I had no answer for a change.

It's a good thing I did send you that quill. Otherwise I would have been filmed using it.

Evil big bro seeing my quill...

I liked the Snargler Spotters' leaflet. They sound like the train spotters we have on Earth.

What work do you do at the
café? I asked my mom if I
could help her with Dawn's
Lawns over the holidays for
extra pocket money, and she
gave me her look.

Then she said she would pay me to stay
away. So much for being ~~enter entrep~~
entrepreneurial. (Why can't letters have
spellcheck? Mrs. Hall you are crazy!!!)

Jon

Class 5U

Flumpenslurp Blurble School

Dome 1

Pluto

                    Fiveday, Fiennes 24th, 2317

Dear Jon,

Wow, you will be on TV! A famous letter writer! Make sure you write Straxi really big when they film you, like this:

And then write about how brilliant I am! Only joking. Just be normal. Be

yourself. Your letters are funny.

You ask what I do at Doolyboppers. I help Dad serve the food Mom makes. It's mostly whirlywangs, which are the best desserts ever.

This one is for you. It's got extra yuffs!

Straxi

Class 5H

Northcroft School

Northcroft

Earth

Tuesday, February 28th, 2317

Dear Straxi,

They are filming right now! As I write!

Mrs. Hall said we can have two

participation points each if we sit still and

write a good letter. My mind is blank.

Now they will be filming me staring into

space like an idiot and my

brother's face will look like

this:

Great. Now I've drawn my brother's face on TV. I'll cover it with my arm if the cameras get nearer. I'm not having HIM getting famous thanks to me.

Oh yes, STRAXI is a great pen pal. She sent me a whirlywang with extra yuffs. There you go. Your name is on TV.

And now the big news. Grandma may get to taste a real whirlywang because she is going to Pluto! She told me about it on a postcard, so she is probably already there. I told her to go to Doolyboppers and said if she sees a pair of twins in

there, you'll be the one holding a quill.

Jon

PS We have just been told to keep

writing because Mrs. Hall is being

interviewed and they want us all working

away in the background. So I will just tell

you that when she saw I'd written <u>Mrs.</u>

<u>Hall YOU ARE CRAZY</u> at the bottom

of my last letter, she TOOK AWAY two

points! And I just realised I wrote it

again, so that'll be two

more.

Flumpenslurp Blurble School

Dome 1

Pluto

Fiveday, Fiennes 24th, 2317

Dear Jon,

Guess what?

Your grandma is sitting right in front
of me in the café! I showed
her the quill and she
wants to see me use it, so
I'm writing my next letter
to you.

I hope I can still write to you now that

you are famous from being on TV. I wish I could watch it, but we only get boring old Channel Pluto, which is mostly documentaries about gardening in low gravity.

Your grandma is great. I can write that now because she's turned away to talk to yes, you guessed it, MY grandma! They have gotten along like a burning yum-yum tree ever since your grandma came into the café for a whirlywang three days ago. She seems to know all about me, too!

Your grandma says to send you her love, and stop fighting with your brother please, and also she's had a whirlywang and they are as good as they look, apart from the extra yuffs, which are not to everyone's taste.

I DISAGREE!

She is going to do a talk at my school about how she got chased by a blarg-ringed flapper surfing on Neptune.

Your gran was surfing, not the flapper. They just lurk under the surfers getting ready to attack.

Your grandma said she only saw one tentacle and a fang, and that was enough.

Straxi

The deadly
Blarg-ringed flapper

Class 5H

Northcroft School

Northcroft

Earth

Tuesday, March 7th, 2317

Dear Straxi,

Sorry that Grandma is going to your school. I am only related to her a little bit, and that is just to the non-crazy part. Was the talk good? Did Grandma show everyone her bite marks?

The WiseUp TV program went out and I looked like a huge snargler in it. We watched it in class, and the only time you see me I am staring into space like my brain has been drained. I knew this would happen. I'm the best letter writer in the class now, but even Rex Smith looks like he's got the hang of it more than me. (He is allowed to write again as long as he sticks to a list of subjects from Mrs. Hall.)

Mrs. Hall said, "The cameras added ten

years and six pounds to me." I said, "You looked like you always do, Mrs. Hall," and I could see her itching to take another two points from me. Then the program showed her collecting the letters to mail them, and you could clearly see the bottom of mine where I wrote Mrs. Hall YOU ARE CRAZY for the second time.

So then she really did take two points from me. Twice.

Jon

Class 5U

Flumpenslurp Blurble School

Dome 1

Pluto

Fiveday, Mallory 3rd, 2317

Dear Jon,

You are a quarter "Crazy Grandma"—
that is more than a little bit related!

Your grandma's talk was great. She is
now a celebrity here. I told you we don't
get many tourists. Everyone blames it
on the vomblefruit, but I think we are
just too far away. The only visitors we

get are scientists and explorers. And crazy grandmas!

Anyway, your grandma really is a celebrity, and not just because she's the only person wearing gravity boots. (We're used to low gravity and wear slightly heavier clothes.)

Yesterday, the President of Pluto took her on a bird-watching trip. They went to see the blue-headed skwitches doing their courtship dance in the Blue Prairies. When they came back to Doolyboppers for a furgel juice afterward, we heard him say, "You are

quite a lady, Doris," even though she'd brought binoculars with her to watch ten feet high birds, which is a bit "Crazy Grandma." Then Bryd said to me, "I bet they get married, don't you?" And it would all be because of us and the letter writing and Mrs. Hall's mission.

Straxi

THE BLUE-HEADED SKWITCH COURTSHIP DANCE

Right leg up

Left leg up

Right leg up

Squawk!

PLUTO NATURE NOTES

One of Pluto's Seven Natural Wonders!

Class 5H

Northcroft School

Northcroft

Earth

Tuesday, March 14th, 2317

Dear Straxi,

Mrs. Hall said the Pluto government are spraying the whole of Pluto with vomblefruit killer. They are going to get rid of vomblefruit once and for all—I can hear you shouting hurray all the way from Pluto four point six seven billion miles away (look Mrs. Hall, I've learned something).

Hurray!

Mrs. Hall says she won't be able to mail my letters because no space shuttles will be going to or from Pluto until the spraying has finished. "Does that mean I can stop writing?" I asked, but Mrs. Hall said, "Absolutely not," and she will save up my letters and mail them all at once later on. So I groaned loudly, but secretly I was pleased because I like hearing about Doolyboppers and Crazy Grandmas and blue-headed skwitches and even snarglers because they are weird but people like them (like my brother).

So I don't know when you will read this. I
don't even know how they can spray a
whole planet.

How big is the can?

Do you have to stay inside, or do you get
sprayed too?

How long does it take?

Jon

Class 5H

Northcroft School

Northcroft

Earth

Tuesday, March 21st 2317

Dear Straxi,

I haven't heard from you, and you haven't heard from me because I'm not allowed to send my letter yet. But it's Language Arts, so here goes.

I watched the news with Dad last night to see if they said anything about Pluto being sprayed, but they didn't. When he

got over the shock of me
watching the news, Dad
explained that the Pluto
people left Earth because
there were too many

Whaaaat?!

wars and they wanted to start again and
be peaceful. And they were right because
I have never heard of a war on Pluto. So
Earth is ignoring them on purpose, like
little sis does when big bro won't play My
Ickle Pickle Dress-Up Princess Pony with
her.

Jon

Class 5H

Northcroft School

Northcroft

Earth

                    Tuesday, March 28th, 2317

Dear Straxi,

I wonder what's happening. How is

Grandma (mine)? The message on the

Visit Pluto website (visitor count 00005)

says you've all got to stay inside for

                    another two weeks.

                    Two weeks!

Are you bored? Have all the vomblefruit
trees gone yet? We still have the
vomblefruit you sent. At first the
greenhouse smelt
awful, but Mom WEIRD!!
filled it with all the
nicest smelling
plants she's got.
Also, I caught
her giving it a
little polish with a cloth.

Mom claims she has masked
the smell, but every so often
I catch a whiff on her

Eau de Vomblefruit

clothes. Eau de Vomblefruit. That's a fancy name for a perfume, if anyone was insane enough to make one out of vomblefruit. It would have to come with a free barf bucket.

I hope you get this letter soon. I don't draw barf buckets just for fun, you know.

Jon

Class 5H

Northcroft School

Northcroft

Earth

Tuesday, April 4th, 2317

Dear Straxi,

What is going on?!

I am writing this imagining you sitting at home waiting until it's safe to go outside.

I wonder what your home looks like? Somewhere that sells whirlywangs with extra yuffs must be pretty crazy—

looking.

Talking of crazy-looking (and acting),
little sis asked big bro to cut her hair. On
one side. Mom said her new hairstyle was
punishment enough. Sis said she was
trying to look like My Ickle Pickle
Dress Up Princess Pony with

Before

a lovely mane. And she
sort of does.

Then Mom said, "That
reminds me, Jon, you need a

After

haircut. You're beginning to
look like a yeti." (That's a

big hairy monster that lives up in the mountains in case you don't have them on Pluto. Actually we don't have them on Earth either. I think they are a myth. Or extinct.)

I said, "Why do I have to be punished too?" and she said, "A haircut isn't a punishment, Jon, it's a treat, and I wish I could spend three hours sitting at the hairdressers, instead of pulling up people's weeds and running around after you kids all day."

THREE HOURS?! What do they do, cut

Flip over

one hair at a time?

I hope you get this letter one day and it doesn't just live in Mrs. Hall's desk forever like Rex Smith's project on belly button fluff. I am sending you a yeti.

Jon

A yeti

Class 5U

Flumpenslurp Blurble School

Dome 1

Pluto

Fiveday, Aldrin 21st, 2317

Dear Jon,

It's me! At last! Thank you for the yeti
and the perfume and the barf bucket.
They arrived all at once! Sorry I couldn't
tell you what was happening. They made
us stay inside because the spray
wouldn't go away. Bryd said it was like a
big old sneeze hanging in the air.

We had to do lessons at home with an

e-teacher. That means the teacher is at
her home and you are YAWWN!
at yours. You can see
her drinking her cup of
buggle-tea and
yawning.

For meals we had to
eat packets of dried space travel food—
yuck! Bryd and I sneaked downstairs to
whirlywangs, but Dad caught us. He said
to save the whirlywangs for the
customers, since everyone will be dying
for a treat when they come out. So we
had to resist. We deserve a medal.

73

Our house is pretty crazy. It has a flashing sign and huge models of food on it. My bedroom has a great view of a giant glowing plastic yuff!

All the vomblefruit trees are dead, every single one. I feel so sad. Everyone is

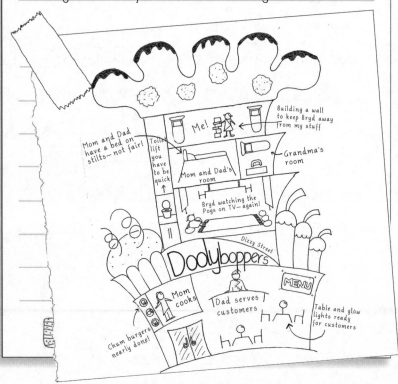

Building a wall to keep Bryd away from my stuff

Mom and Dad have a bed on stilts— not fair!

Me!

Toilet lift you have to be quick

Grandma's room

Mom and Dad's room

Bryd watching the Pogs on TV— again!

Dizzy Street

Doodyboppers

Mom cooks

Dad serves customers

MENU

Table and glow lights ready for customers

Chum burgers nearly done!

celebrating, saying tourists will come and bring money to Pluto, and then we can build more domes and farms.

But I miss the vomblefruit trees. They were so beautiful, even though the fruit smelled worse than a yeti's armpit.

Straxi

PS Thank you for still writing to me, even though I wasn't writing back.

PPS I drew you a meal from Doolyboppers and a picture of my house.

PPPS And I wondered if you knew what was happening and if you were thinking about me.

PPPPS You were! You drew me a yeti and some perfume and a barf bucket!

Chum Burger

JON'S SPECIAL MEAL AT DOOLYBOPPERS

Dizzy St, Pluto

Served by the best waitress in the Solar
System, Straxi Dooly!

APPETIZER

Bugglecrumpet with Melto-Lac cheese and

smippo dip

ENTRÉE

Plip legs and ri tentacles on a bed of wriggle-
shrimps (Only joking, chum burger of course!)

DESSERT

Whirlywang surprise
(The surprise is it's double size!)
Best shared with a twin. Or pen pal.

Class 5H

Northcroft School

Northcroft

Earth

Tuesday, April 25th, 2317

Dear Straxi,

Thanks for the meal. And thanks for not making me eat ri tentacles. Chum burger sounds much nicer (I think).

I've been showing everyone the picture of your house. Grandma (mine) is lucky being on Pluto. I wish I had a toilet lift and dinner on the ceiling.

We got a postcard from Grandma (mine)

today too. I'm writing back to both of you

at the same time—well, one

after the other, not one with

each hand at once. No,

I'm writing TWO

letters today. And I'm

not even at school. Mrs. Hall would

probably die of happiness if she saw me.

I looked up Pluto online. Bit bare, isn't it?

Jon

PS   Now I have   I'm sooooooo happy!!

to write to Grandma.

PPS She'll want to hear I've been doing something exciting and risk-taking, like her.

PPPS I had to look through the lost and found bin for my PE shorts on Thursday.

PPPPS I'll tell her about that.

LOST &
FOUND

Class 5U

Flumpenslurp Blurble School

Dome 1

Pluto

Fiveday, Aldrin 28th, 2317

Dear Jon,

We don't eat dinner on the ceiling! It's a pull-down table and chairs to save space. Don't you have furniture on the ceiling?

It does look bare here. And it's so quiet. It's not just the squelch of falling fruit that's missing or the sound of people going, "Yuck!"

The birds are quieter
too. I walked right
past a blue-headed
skwitch yesterday, and
he just looked at me
as if to say, "Oh
humans, what have
you done?" But Mom
said it was probably
just looking down at
my shoes, which are
fluorescent yellow and
tasty-looking to birds.

Sad skwitch

So I went upstairs to do my homework,
but I kept looking out of the window,

and there were no blue-headed skwitches nesting in the yum-yum tree anymore and I couldn't even make an imaginary one in my head.

Straxi

My yellow shoes

Class 5H

Northcroft School

Northcroft

Earth

Tuesday, May 2nd, 2317

Dear Straxi,

You have fluorescent yellow shoes?

Maybe they are normal on Pluto. Tip:

they are not normal here.

Don't worry about the birds. They

probably just didn't like the spray. If it

really was like a big sneeze hanging in

the air, I don't blame them.

We have no furniture on the ceiling. There is some tomato sauce there where little sis shook the bottle without putting the lid back on first. I wonder how long it will stay there, or if one day it will drip down on big bro's head?

Got another postcard from Grandma (mine). She said she might be coming home soon. Can you ask her to bring a menu from Doolyboppers? And a feather. I know you can't mail one, as they are

I hope it lands on big bro

six feet long, but surely one would fit on
a spaceship?

Mrs. Hall just peered over my shoulder.
Now she's asking me to finish my letter
and go and help Rex Smith. I don't know
if that's a reward or a punishment.

Jon

You carrying
a feather

A feather
carrying you

Class 5U

Flumpenslurp Blurble School

Dome 1

Pluto

Fiveday, McArthur 5th, 2317

Dear Jon,

The birds have stopped singing. There is

no green anywhere; it's all brown and

dying. I was right to feel sad. The blue-

headed skwitch liked vomblefruit and it

doesn't want to eat anything else.

They said on Pluto News that its

trailing feathers spread pollen around.

Now none of the other plants are

growing either. Even our yum-yum tree has gone all droopy.

Lots of people are leaving. Your grandma's decided to stay and help. She has a meeting with the President. I don't think they are going on dates anymore. Everything is too serious for that.

My quill has run out. It doesn't feel the same.

Straxi

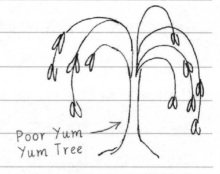

Poor Yum Yum Tree

Class 5H

Northcroft School

Northcroft

Earth

Tuesday, May 9th, 2317

Dear Straxi,

I just saw Pluto on the news! I asked Dad

why they were finally showing stuff about

Pluto, and he said it was a disaster now,

so it's more interesting and also people

are saying I told you so because the

Pluto Project is a failure. I asked him

what the Pluto Project was, and he said it

was about freedom and also the

challenge of survival in a harsh

environment. I think he means like the moldy shower at school. No one wants to go in there because it smells, but Rex Smith stayed in there for ten minutes and got respect.

I asked Mrs. Hall where she got the quill from, and she said she would get me another one. But now that people are leaving Pluto, maybe you'll come to Earth soon?

I bet you'll like it. We don't have weird buildings like you do, or giant birds, and you might not want to wear fluorescent yellow shoes. And the gravity will be different. And my brother lives here.

Hang on, that's just going to put you off.

We do have some cool animals here.

Sharks are great. And crocodiles. I like

anything that chases people and bites

them. Apart from my brother, of course.

Pluto can't really be dying. Can it?

Jon

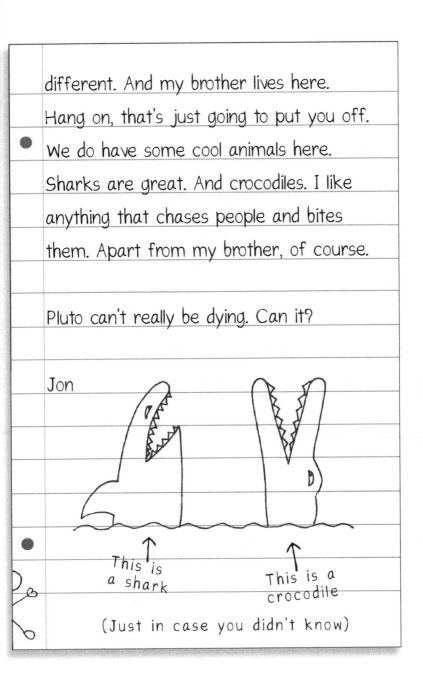

This is
a shark

This is a
crocodile

(Just in case you didn't know)

Class 5U

Flumpenslurp Blurble School

Dome 1

Pluto

Fiveday, McArthur 12th, 2317

Dear Jon,

Mom and Dad have had to close
Doolyboppers. Everyone is leaving and
too busy packing and booking their
flights to come in and eat whirlywangs.

Dad doesn't want to go straight to
Earth. He says we'll go to Neptune first
and see the blarg-ringed flapper, and
then we'll visit Uranus and do a tour of

the moons. They made it sound so exciting, and I've always wanted to leave Pluto and travel, but now I don't want to go.

Pimpam

I was going to be the first zoologist on Pluto and have real pimpams and a fully trained zork. And Bryd was going to make wangywhirls, which are like upside-down whirlywangs, but they won't work in heavier gravity. Nothing on Pluto will work anywhere else. It's our home. Everyone hated the vomblefruit trees when they were here. We didn't know they were keeping everything else alive.

The President says the spray was too good. There isn't one single vomblefruit left. They can't even plant any seeds to grow them again.

He has told your grandma to go home. Bryd says they can't get married now and they are star-crossed lovers. That means fate is keeping them apart, though I know it's really vomblefruit.

We have invited your grandma to come to Neptune with us. I think she wants to get revenge on the blarg-ringed flapper.

Straxi

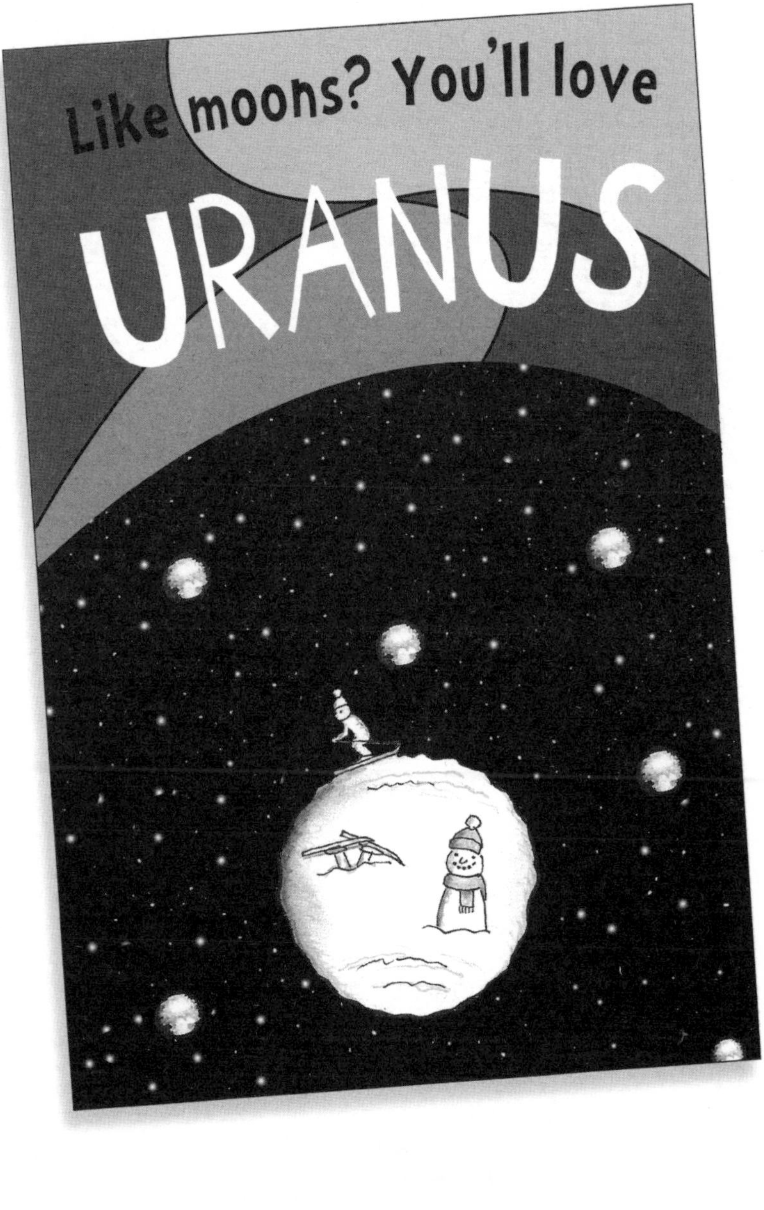
Like moons? You'll love
URANUS

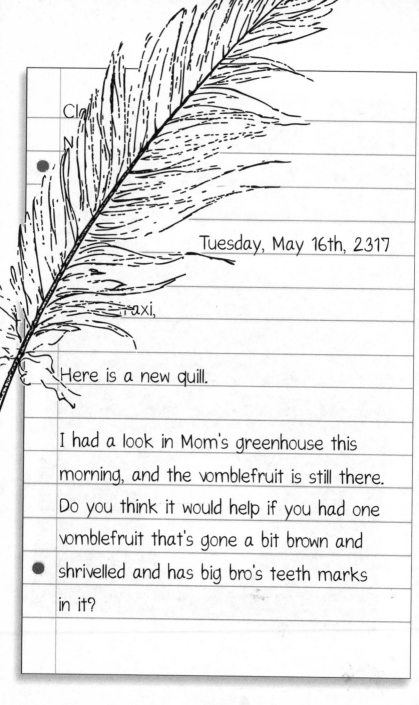

Cl...

N...

Tuesday, May 16th, 2317

...axi,

Here is a new quill.

I had a look in Mom's greenhouse this
morning, and the vomblefruit is still there.
Do you think it would help if you had one
vomblefruit that's gone a bit brown and
shrivelled and has big bro's teeth marks
in it?

96

I asked Mrs. Hall to mail this immediately when I've finished. She gave me a sickly smile and said, "The way you have taken this project to heart, Jon, makes all the years I have put into my teaching career worthwhile."

"Surely that's worth a few points," I said. "We'll see," she said in a cunning tone that is meant to bribe me into being good.

Jon

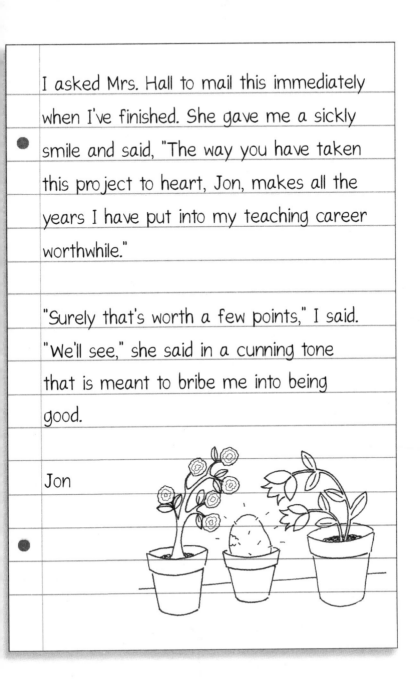

FBS

Dome 1

Pluto

McArthur 19th

Dear Jon,

Yes! Yes! Yes!

Get the seed out of the middle of the vomblefruit (hold your nose)! Send it to me! Hurry!

Straxi

Same old school

Same old planet

Dear Straxi

The seed is in with this letter. I don't

know how to wrap it so I've just taped it

to the paper. It's glowing. Hope that's

normal. Also, it doesn't really smell much

anymore—guess Mom's stinky plants

helped.

I'm posting this myself because I didn't

want to wait for school. Some things are

more important than

SHOCK HORROR!

Language Arts.

Mrs. Hall must never read that last
sentence.

Jon

FBS

Dome 1

Pluto

McArthur 26th

Dear Jon,

The seed's arrived! With a police escort! Flashing lights, sirens, and everything! I can't believe you did all that! The President hasn't planted it yet. They are trying to decide the best site and they are going to fence it off and have a guard around it day and night. Pluto News is filming everything! Got to go!

Straxi

Still here

Earth

Tuesday, May 30th, 2317

Dear Straxi,

I didn't arrange anything! I mailed the
letter to you with the seed, and when I
got back Mom was weeding the front
garden and said, "Isn't it sad about Pluto?"
I said I'd sent you the seed and she said,
"Eek! That might just work!" but when I
said I'd just sent it in an envelope she
said, "Eek!" again and called our state
representative and he called the
President. Yes, really!

Then the President sent police around to escort the seed to Pluto, which sounds important and exciting, but the problem was it was still in the mailbox so the police just had to stand around the mailbox until the mail carrier could come and unlock it and get the envelope out.

Then a police helicopter came down and took up the envelope with the seed in it, and the police went too, and the mail carrier was accidentally lifted up in the helicopter as well. I could see him waving and shouting, but I think he actually enjoyed it.

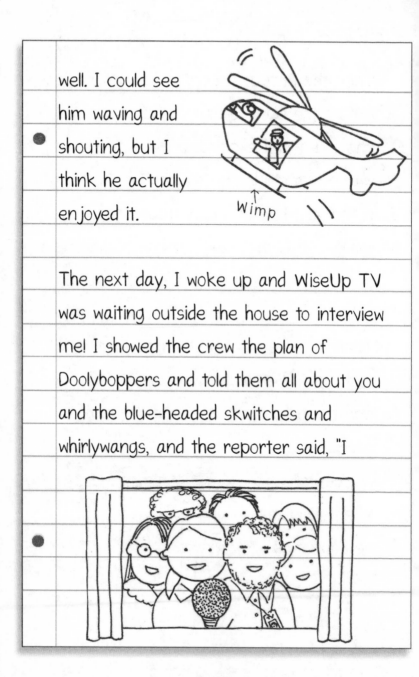

Wimp

The next day, I woke up and WiseUp TV was waiting outside the house to interview me! I showed the crew the plan of Doolyboppers and told them all about you and the blue-headed skwitches and whirlywangs, and the reporter said, "I didn't know Pluto was so interesting, son, I would like to go there some day." And I said I would too. Then he turned to the camera and said in a dramatic voice, "Can one boy save life on Pluto?" which I thought was a bit over the top, and even more so when we watched it later and you could see Mom putting her arm

WHY?!

around me and sad music playing in the background while they zoomed in on my dumb face.

I know everyone's supposed to want to be famous, but now that I am, I can tell you that fame is just one big embarrassing moment. With witnesses.

Jon

FBS

Dome 1

Pluto

Fiveday, Johnson 3rd, 2317

Dear Jon,

Every day I walk to the planting site. It is surrounded by police from Earth and Guardians, which is the name for our police on Pluto.

There is a special dome over the seed to protect it and a giant video screen showing a close-up view. I don't think so many people have ever spent so long

looking at nothing.

A lot of
people are
still leaving
for other planets. Some say the seed
won't grow, and other people say the
birds will carry on dying anyway. I want
to grab everyone and say, "Give the seed
a chance!" But Bryd stopped me doing
that because she said it was
embarrassing.

I think I'll go and look at the seed again.
I'll stand with the skwitches. They have
the best view.

The reporter was right—if it works, we will have SAVED PLUTO!

Straxi

Where?
Over here!
Earth

June 6th, 2317

Dear Straxi,

Reporters are camped outside the house filming my every move. Mom got piles of new clothes and had a five hour haircut. Dad took a camera apart for fun and

5 HOURS?!

now the reporters don't like him very much. Little sis is putting on a show with her toy ponies, and big bro has stopped chasing me because he doesn't want to look bad on TV in front of his new girlfriend. So things are good. Weird, but good.

Except for one thing. Mrs. Hall is trying to get a bunch more schools to write to pen pals on other planets and wants me to be an Ambassador of Handwriting.

"What's that?" I asked.

"It means you would be the face of my campaign."

"No thanks," I said, "I would rather eat vomblefruit for breakfast, lunch, and dinner." Turns out I have no choice and, "It will mean extra points, Jon, and you know how you like those."

Teacher's pet at last, how I have changed. I will go and tie my brother's shoelaces to the chair leg to make up for it.

And then I'll go and watch the seed on the news.

You can stop filming now, I've finished.

That bit was for the reporters, not you.

I SAID I'VE FINISHED!

Nope, they're going to come with me to the mailbox. The burden of being a celebrity.

Jon

PS Come on seed, you can do it!

FBS

Dome 1

Pluto

Fiveday, Johnson 9th, 2317

Dear Jon,

Lots of people have left Pluto now. Only the people who weren't sure, like Mom and Dad, are holding on just in case.

Everyone who's still here is visiting the seed, but it's me, Bryd, and the Crazy Grandmas who are there the most.

More and more skwitches are standing around near the planting site. I think

they are waiting and hoping, just like us.
If we can stay on Pluto, I would like to
study them. I might even go and live in
a flock for a while. Bryd says I'm weird,
but that's what I would like to do. And I
already have the shoes.

Yes, I did say Crazy Grandmas with an

s. Your grandma refused to leave. She says she can help and besides, she likes the vibe here. "What's that?" I asked. "Is it a nickname for the President?" since she sometimes calls him funny names like sugar. She blushed and said, "No, it's something everyone has on Pluto, and it makes me want to stay."

I wonder if all grandmas are crazy or if it's just ours.

I got the seed a present. It's a little pebble from the Glowing Canyon. I'm going to

put it just
outside the dome
so it has to
stretch out of its
little hole to see it.

Off to the planting site now. Wish you
could come with me.

Straxi

PS   Just got back—it's poking out of
the ground! And it has two leaves! We
did it! We did it! Running to the
mailbox right now!!!

Guess...

Yes! Earth!

June 13th, 2317

Dear Straxi,

We did it! We really did it!

So this is the last letter I will write to you. At least for a while. Because... I'M COMING TO PLUTO!

"How?" "When?" "Why?" you are asking. Well, stop asking and I'll tell you.

WiseUp TV came to school yesterday to

interview me about how our letters have saved Pluto (nearly). But your letters were at home and mine were on Pluto so that was going to be a very short show.

Then Mrs. Hall rushed over to her laptop, and it turns out she scans in everybody's letters before she sends them so she can mark our spelling and punctuation. Nosiness is what I call it.

She won't like reading that. Sorry, Mrs. Hall. Anyway, I don't care because

I'M COMING TO PLUTO!

So, after they had filmed pieces of the letters and I saw my pictures of perfume bottles and you on a feather, I wished I could disappear. But then the

reporter handed me an envelope, and inside were round-trip tickets to Pluto, and there were five. One each for me, Mom, Dad, big bro, and little sis. I tried to drop my brother's ticket on the floor, but the reporter thought it had slipped out of my hand in all the excitement and gave it back to me.

We are coming out next week! WiseUp TV is coming too, and the crew wants to film me and you standing in front of the tiny tree. IT'S A TREE!

Earth news is showing loads of Pluto stuff now. They said they are going to follow the story and Earth is going to do more to support Pluto, even though the Pluto people left Earth to start again on their own. And then they showed the President of Pluto saying forgive and forget, and I saw Grandma (mine) next to him wearing her "Hello Earth" T-shirt, and I saw two twins waving like crazy and one was holding a quill and I knew it was you.

Jon

↑
You

THE SOLAR TIMES

Pluto edition

Max 78° F, min 48° F   Johnson 19ᵗʰ, 2317 $1.50

SEED OF FRIENDSHIP SAVES "PLANET" PLUTO

Pen pals plot a plan to transport Pluto seed!

Jon (Earth) and Straxi (Pluto) save the "planet" of Pluto when they plot a plan to mail the last vomblefruit seed in existence from Jon's greenhouse back to Pluto.

Pluto's president had decided to eradicate the smelly vomblefruit trees in hopes that it would increase tourism. "It was a plan that the whole planet supported," the President said, "but we had no idea that it would have such a drastic impact on our ecosystem."

When the "planet" was on the brink of desertion, young Jon and Straxi came to the rescue. Story continues on page 7.

Blarg-ringed flapper attacks are on the rise

Neptune coast guard reports an increase in the vicious attacks from the native Blarg-ringed flapper that lurks near Neptune's popular beaches.

"We've seen a rise in attacks in the last few months and predict more for the summer." says chief of police, Robert Urn, "it is tough to put precautions in place due to the creatures' lurking tendencies."

We spoke to a Blarg-ringed flapper suvivor, Mrs. Fisher from Earth, to find out more about these attacks. Here is her story:

"I was surfing at Ariel Beach, which by the way is the best beach for surfing in Neptune, when out of nowhere, I was. . .

FASHION & BEAUTY
Stylish Anti-Gravity Boots
u de Vomblefruit: The
of Perfume?

COMMUNITY
Whirlywangs - to yuff or not to yuff?
Adopt a Skwitch!

The End

Jon's first whirlywang!

Fisher family selfie!

Crazy grandmas selfie!

Lil sis meets a skwitch

Photobomb!

Brothers and sisters selfie

Classic!

It's a tree!!

Northcroft School

Northcroft

Earth

Tuesday, June 21st, 2317

Dear Jon,

I have not received your first letter yet, but I am
hoping you enjoyed your flight to Pluto. Why don't
you write and tell me about it using lots of describing
words?

Mrs. Hall

Northcroft School

Northcroft

Earth

Tuesday, June 28th, 2317

Dear Jon,

I am disappointed not to have received a letter from you yet. I know the solar postal system is slow, but Rex Smith still managed to receive his weekly jigsaw piece from Uranus. (How he thinks he and his pen pal can do a jigsaw together by mail is beyond me.) I look forward to hearing all about your first week.

Mrs. Hall

Northcroft School

Northcroft

Earth

Tuesday, July 5th, 2317

Dear Jon,

I have just seen you on Solar System News eating a whirlywang. Please send me your first letter or I will take away 2 points, which will be very difficult because you don't have any. I am enclosing a homework timetable. And don't forget to write a holiday diary. And a thank you letter to the TV people. You are my Ambassador of Handwriting now, remember? I hope you are actually reading this, Jon. Jon?

Mrs. Hall